4 5 billion years ago, our planet, Earth, forms.

3 1 billion years after the Big Bang, the galaxies begin to take shape.

8 2.5 billion years ago, our breathable atmosphere forms.

7 3 billion years ago, life begins with the appearance of the first bacteria and blue algae.

Tyrannosaurus

Argentinosaurus

Baryonyx

Vol. 6

Triceratops

Vol. 5

Camarasaurus

Vol. 4

Giganotosaurus

Scipionyx

Cretaceous

CONTENTS

First published in the United States of America in 2010 by
Abbeville Press, 137 Varick Street, New York, NY 10013

First published in Italy in 2010 by Editoriale Jaca Book S.p.A.,
via Frua 11, 20146 Milano

First edition
10 9 8 7 6 5 4 3 2 1

Library of Congress Cataloging-in-Publication Data

Bacchin, Matteo.
[Crepuscolo degli dei. English]
T. rex and the great extinction / drawings and story, Matteo
Bacchin ;
essays Marco Signore ; translated from the Italian by
Marguerite Shore. --
1st ed.
p. cm. -- (Dinosaurs)
ISBN 978-0-7892-1014-2 (hardcover : alk. paper)
1. Dinosaurs--Extinction--Juvenile literature. 2.
Paleontology--Cretaceous--Juvenile literature. I. Signore,
Marco. II.
Title.
QE861.6.E95B3313 2010
567.9--dc22
2010021123

For bulk and premium sales and for text adoption procedures,
write to Customer Service Manager, Abbeville Press, 137 Varick
Street, New York, NY 10013, or call 1-800-ARTBOOK.

Visit Abbeville Press online at www.abbeville.com.

For the English-language edition: Amy K. Hughes, editor;
Ashley Benning, copy editor; Louise Kurtz, production manager;
Guenet Abraham, composition; Ada Blazer, cover design.

Foreword
By Mark Norell

Imagine a warm, humid evening in a swampy forest in what is now western North America. Flocks of *Triceratops* graze on low plants, as insects buzz and tyrannosaurs linger under tall trees. Then the sky brightens and—*bang*—a giant asteroid about 3.5 miles across has collided with Earth some 3,000 miles to the south. The immense amount of energy released causes the atmosphere to radiate. The effects will be felt for years, with darkened skies, cataclysmic fires, acid rain, and global catastrophe. In an instant the world has changed, the dinosaurs have vanished, and an ecosystem has collapsed. Or has it?

This is the debate that has raged for nearly 30 years. On one side stand the catastrophists, who, ever since evidence for the extraterrestrial strike was discovered, have pointed to this single cause for the destruction of the Cretaceous world. All the evidence says that this was a very bad day for Earth. A gross reading of the fossil record shows that all sorts of species became extinct. In addition to the dinosaurs, organisms as disparate as plants and clams were affected. Our best fossil record is the aquatic one, in which wholesale disruption of the biota occurred. Ammonites (relatives of the nautilus) disappeared, and there was a decrease in the number of echinoderm, mollusk, and even plankton species.

But was it really that bad, and what does a very fine reading of the fossil record tell us? First, as you have read in these books, dinosaur extinction is something of a misnomer. Dinosaurs did not all become extinct; today we call them birds. Only some dinosaurs died out 65.5 million years ago. Furthermore, most of the evidence suggests that non-avian dinosaurs were decreasing in diversity millions of years before the impact, perhaps as the result of volcanic activity, climate change, and the drying up of intercontinental seas. The same is true of other reptiles, such as the pterosaurs and crocodilians. Also, the terrestrial fossil record is simply not that good, so it is hard to tell if animals like the non-avian dinosaurs disappeared before the impact or at it. The data are very difficult to analyze, and the amazing thing is that so many animals (such as our mammalian ancestors, the birds, and every other major animal and plant group alive today) survived the impact.

While everyone agrees that the asteroid impact was a very significant event in Earth's history, it alone does not explain the demise of the dinosaurs nor the entire pattern of extinction at the end of the Cretaceous.

T. REX AND THE GREAT EXTINCTION

For their help and support both direct and indirect Matteo Bacchin would like to thank (in no particular order) Marco Signore; Luis V. Rey; Francesca Belloni; Sante Bagnoli; Joshua Volpara; and his dear friends Mac, Stefano, Lorenzo M., Giorgio, Donato, Lorenzo R., and Giacinto. But he thanks above all his mother, his father, and Greta, for the unconditional love, support, and feedback that have allowed him to realize this dream.

Marco Signore would like to thank his parents, his family, Marilena, Enrico di Torino, Sara, his Chosen Ones (Claudio, Rino, Vincenzo), Luis V. Rey, Matteo Bacchin, and everybody who has believed in him.

DINOSAURS

T. Rex and the Great Extinction

Drawings and story
MATTEO BACCHIN

Essays
MARCO SIGNORE

Comics colored by
N.L.C. Srl–Cinisello B.Mo. (MI)

Translated from the Italian
by Marguerite Shore

ABBEVILLE KIDS
A Division of Abbeville
Publishing Group
New York London

IN THIS STORY

(Meters)

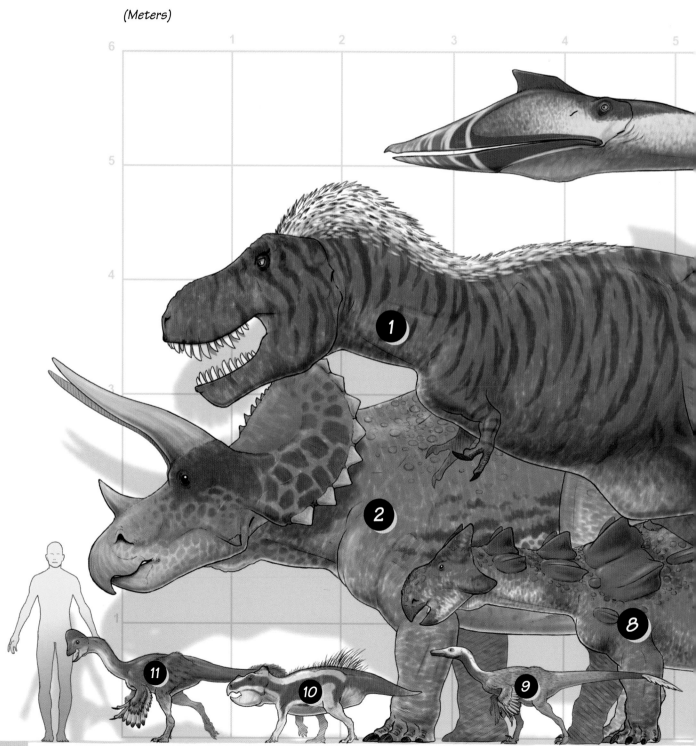

1 Tyrannosaurus 4 Edmontosaurus 8 Ankylosaurus

2 Triceratops 5 Ornithomimus 9 Troodon

3 Quetzalcoatlus 6 Stygimoloch 10 Leptoceratops

7 Torosaurus 11 Chirostenotes

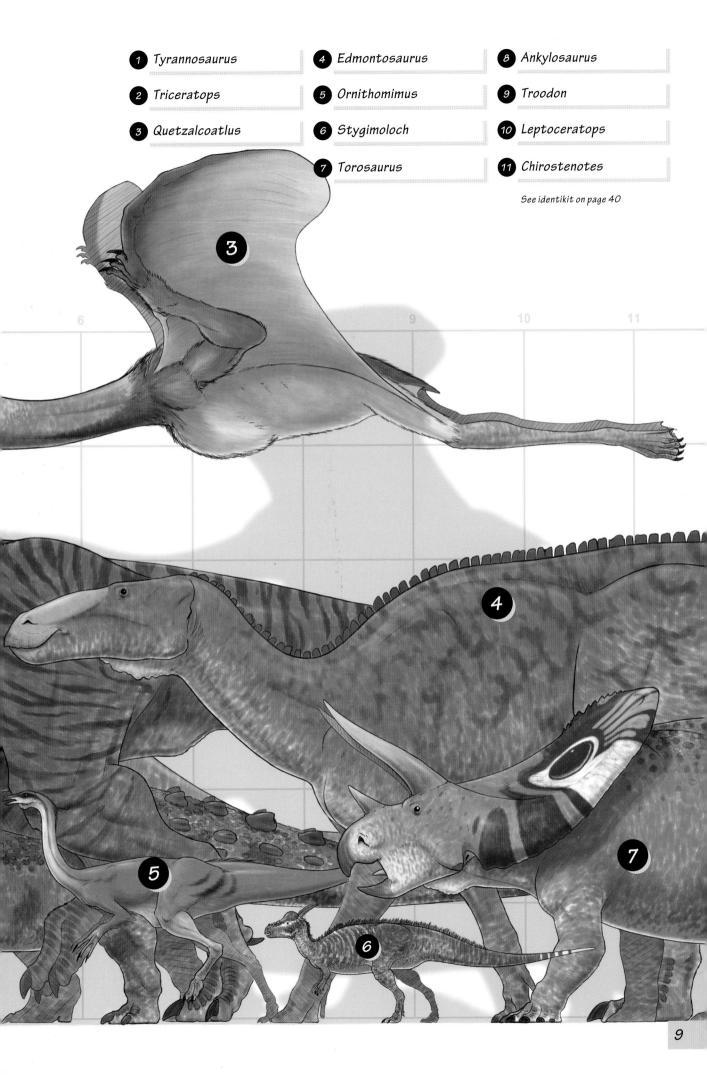

See identikit on page 40

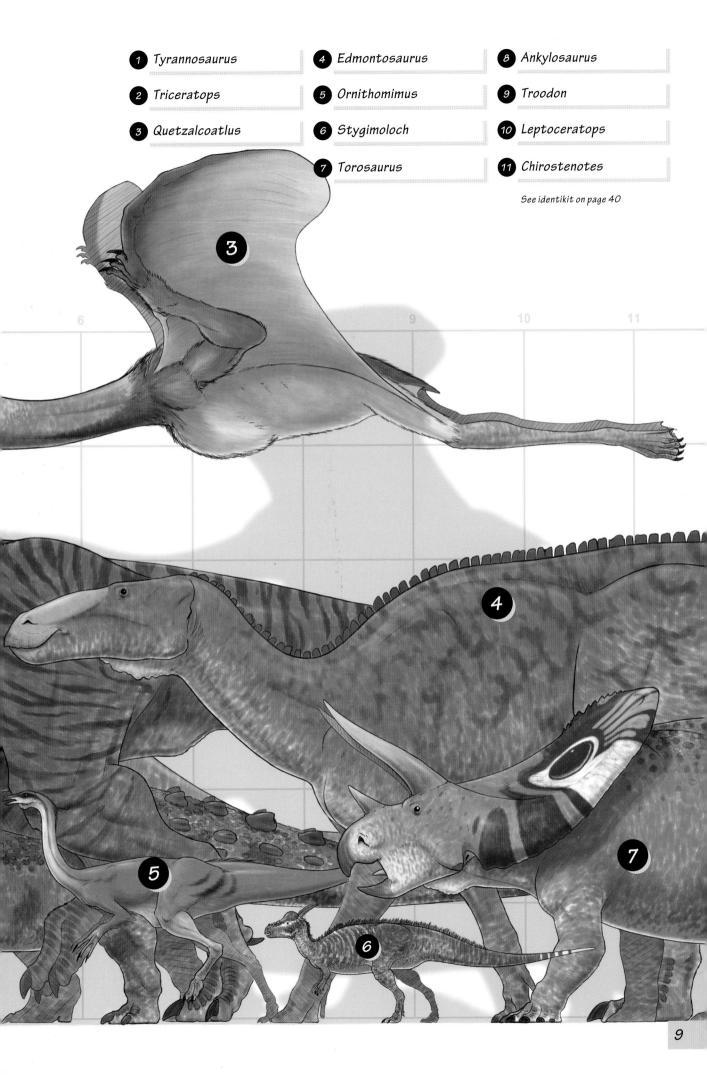

THE NARRATOR

LET ME INTRODUCE MYSELF: I AM A SUN. A YELLOW SUN.

ALTHOUGH I AM NOT THE LARGEST AMONG ALL THE STARS, I HAVE SEEN MANY THINGS, MUCH, MUCH MORE THAN MOST OF MY SIBLINGS THAT POPULATE THE CREATOR-COSMOS.

IN FACT, I AM EXTREMELY FORTUNATE: I DO NOT WANDER ALONE IN THIS SEA OF SPACE. VARIOUS PLANETS HAVE BEEN BORN AROUND ME, AND I HAVE BEEN ABLE TO OBSERVE AND WITNESS MANY DIFFERENT LIVES IN THE TIME I HAVE BEEN GRANTED THUS FAR.

AND IT IS PRECISELY ONE VERY GRAND AND UNREPEATABLE PERIOD THAT I AM GOING TO TELL YOU ABOUT: A MARVEL OF LIFE THAT THE FERTILE EARTH—THE THIRD PLANET AND JEWEL AMONG ALL THE OTHERS—WAS ABLE TO HELP NURTURE AND ALLOW TO THRIVE.

YOU HUMANS HAVE BEEN ABLE TO DISCOVER LOST MEMORIES OF THIS AMAZING PERIOD—IN ROCK AMID ROCKS, STONE EVIDENCE OF THAT PAST ERA AND THE RACE OF CREATURES THAT LIVED THEN.

TIME HAS TURNED THEM INTO SILENT STONES AND EMPTIED THEIR CHESTS OF BREATH AND WARMTH.

THEIR EMPTY EYE SOCKETS STILL SEEM TO PROBE, PIERCING YOU AS YOU CONTEMPLATE THEM IN THE HALLS OF MUSEUMS, AND HYPNOTIZING YOU WHILE YOU TRY TO PEER, THROUGH THOSE PETRIFIED WINDOWS, INTO THE TWISTS AND TURNS OF THEIR ANCESTRAL ERAS.

DISTANT ERAS, WHOSE LEGEND WAS ALREADY FORGOTTEN BEFORE THE PYRAMIDS AND THE SPHINX, BEFORE FIRE, BEFORE THE STONE AGE.

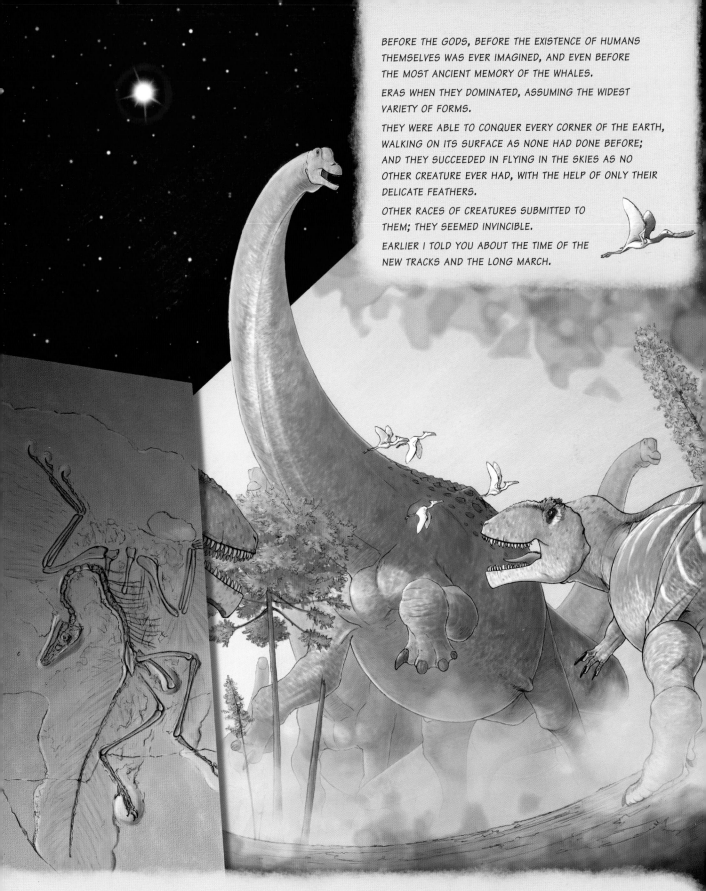

BEFORE THE GODS, BEFORE THE EXISTENCE OF HUMANS THEMSELVES WAS EVER IMAGINED, AND EVEN BEFORE THE MOST ANCIENT MEMORY OF THE WHALES.

ERAS WHEN THEY DOMINATED, ASSUMING THE WIDEST VARIETY OF FORMS.

THEY WERE ABLE TO CONQUER EVERY CORNER OF THE EARTH, WALKING ON ITS SURFACE AS NONE HAD DONE BEFORE; AND THEY SUCCEEDED IN FLYING IN THE SKIES AS NO OTHER CREATURE EVER HAD, WITH THE HELP OF ONLY THEIR DELICATE FEATHERS.

OTHER RACES OF CREATURES SUBMITTED TO THEM; THEY SEEMED INVINCIBLE.

EARLIER I TOLD YOU ABOUT THE TIME OF THE NEW TRACKS AND THE LONG MARCH.

I TOLD YOU ABOUT THE ERA OF ASCENT: HOW THE ANCIENT WINGED CREATURE BECAME MYTH, AND THE YOUNG RIVAL SUCCEEDED THE ANCIENT LEADER OF THE PACK OF THREE-CLAWED CREATURES.

AND I TOLD YOU ABOUT A LATER TIME: ABOUT THE EGG, THE NEST, AND THE ADULT CREATURE, AND THE EXTRAORDINARY DAILY LIFE OF THE TITANS OF PATAGONIA.

OUR JOURNEY THROUGH THE ERAS OF THEIR EXISTENCE HAS ALREADY WOUND THROUGH FIVE STORIES, AND ONLY ONE REMAINS NOW AT THE END OF THIS PATH OF MEMORY. LET ME TELL YOU NOW ABOUT THE KING, AND HOW HE VIEWED THE WINTER OF HIS REIGN AND THE CREATURES THAT INHABITED IT. THESE ARE THE LAST OF THEIR KIND, AND IT IS THEY ALONE WHO KNOW THE SECRET FATE OF THEIR RACE.

I WILL TELL YOU ABOUT...

THE DINOSAURS

6 T. REX AND THE GREAT EXTINCTION

BUT THIS WORLD, SO FAMILIAR AS IT PREPARES FOR ITS WINTER SLEEP, IS NOT THE WORLD OF HUMANS.

NO TIGER OR BEAR OR WOLF HAS DOMINION OVER THIS VAST REALM.

FWAP

THE MASTER OF THE NORTH HAS LONG, MIGHTY LEGS...

...THE BODY OF A WARRIOR...

...A POWERFUL NECK, AND A GIGANTIC HEAD ARMED WITH FIERCE FANGS.

HE IS THE KING OF THE DINOSAURS.

HE IS TYRANT OVER AN ANCIENT BUT INCREASINGLY MODERN REALM: THE WORLD OF THE LAST DINOSAURS, THE ERA OF THE SPECTACULAR DECLINE OF THE FEARSOME LIZARDS, THE UNFORESEEN TWILIGHT OF THE GODS.

15

THE KING KEEPS A STATELY PACE.

HE ADVANCES SILENTLY, SURVEYING HIS ENDLESS TERRITORY.

HE DOES NOT HURRY AND DOES NOT FEAR THE COLD; HIS BREATH WARMS HIS BELLY.

HIS SNOUT POINTS DOWNWIND. HIS SENSITIVE SENSE OF SMELL HAS PICKED UP A TRACE CARRIED BY THE BREATH OF WINTER.

FWAP

FWAP

FWAP

FWAP

THE KING KNOWS THIS ODOR WELL.

IT IS NOT THE SCENT OF THE SWIFT RUNNERS A SHORT DISTANCE AWAY, WHO GROW RIGID AT THE SIGHT OF HIM.

DESPITE THE WINTER, THE NORTHERN FOREST IS BOUNDLESS AND FLOURISHING.

THE SEASON OF THE SNOWS SUBMERGES ALL IN A MYSTERIOUS SILENCE—PETRIFYING EVERYTHING IN ITS SINISTER WHITENESS.

AND YET ACTIVITY, SLOWED BY FROST, DOES NOT END ENTIRELY.

AS IN THE PAST, THE FORESTS OF THE ERA OF THE LAST DINOSAURS OFFER SHELTER TO MANY CREATURES.

LOOKING LIKE A BIZARRE CROSS BETWEEN A BOAR AND A TROPICAL BIRD, THE HOOKED-BEAK BEAST IS ONE WHO DOES NOT MIGRATE IN WINTER.

ONE IS DIGGING IN SEARCH OF SUCCULENT TUBERS.

RASP

RASP

RASP

RASP

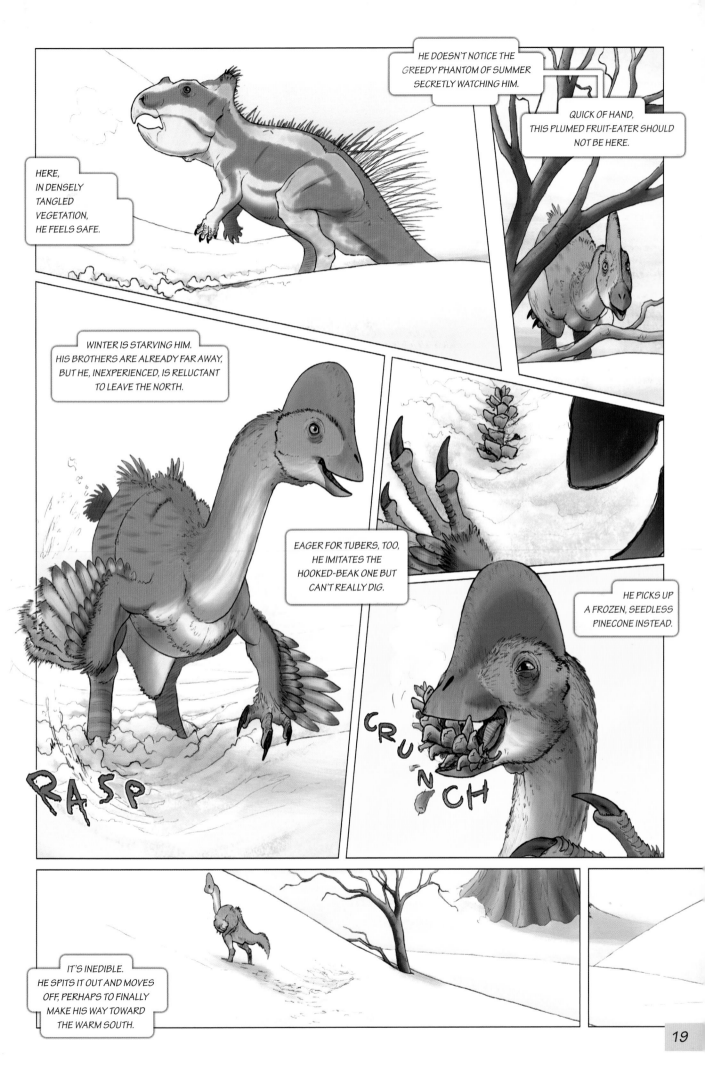

21

HE DESCENDS TO THE RIVER, IGNORING THEIR DISSENT.

HIS DANGEROUS CLAWS SINK INTO THE UNTOUCHED SNOW, CUTTING ITS SURFACE.

HE IS HUNGRY, AND THE GROWING ODOR IS INCREASING HIS APPETITE.

THERE IS LIFE DOWN THERE, NEXT TO SOME FRONDS. BUT THAT IS NOT WHAT IS LURING HIM ON.

LIKE ALL CREATURES, THE KING IS WISE IN HIS WAY, AND HE KNOWS THE ARMORED-BELLIED CREATURES WILL RESPECT HIS DOMINION OVER THE REGION, IF HE RESPECTS THEIRS OVER THAT SMALL GARDEN.

HEAVILY PROTECTED AND LETHALLY ARMED, THEIR BODILY FORM DECLARES THEIR CREED: LIVE AND LET LIVE.

FWAP

ON THE BANK,
LYING AS IF AWKWARDLY THROWN TO THE
GROUND, IS A DUCKBILL'S
LIFELESS BODY.

THE SNOW
HAS TURNED TO
MUD HERE WHERE ITS
FELLOWS
HAVE TRAMPLED THE
EARTH TO CROSS
THE RIVER.

THE VEGETARIAN'S
DARK SKIN STANDS
OUT AGAINST
THE WHITENESS OF ITS
ICY SHROUD.

A GROUP OF EMACIATED
LITTLE SHARP-EYED
DINOSAURS, COVERED WITH
FEATHERS,
FEASTS ON THE HEAD.

ABOVE THEM
GLIDES A MAJESTIC
PLUMED SERPENT,
PERHAPS ALSO DRAWN TO
THE ODOR OF DEATH.

ILLNESS OR ACCIDENT,
THE CAUSE OF DEATH IS NOT FOR
THEM TO KNOW.

FWAP FWAP

IT DOES NOT
MATTER TO THE
KING.

THE SLENDER
PLUMED ONES
SLIP OFF LIKE
THIEVES, MOVING
TO A RESPECTFUL
DISTANCE.

THE TYRANT
BITES INTO THE BODY.

AND WHILE THE HUNTER
BEGINS HIS MEAL,
IN DREAMLIKE QUIET . . .

A DELICATE SNOW
FALLS FROM THE LEADEN SKY.

25

SOME DAYS LATER, STREAKS OF SKY PENETRATE THE BLANKET OF CLOUDS.

A LONE ARMORED DINOSAUR BREAKFASTS ON AN EVERGREEN SHRUB.

THE COLD MAKES IT TOUGHER THAN USUAL . . .

. . . BUT THE ROBUST, GNARLED DINOSAUR DOES NOT MIND.

A HERD OF DUCKBILLS THAT IS CROSSING THE VALLEY, MOVING SOUTH, ALSO KNOWS TO GIVE A WIDE BERTH TO THE ARMORED CREATURE AND ITS HARD SPIKES.

THE PLUMED SERPENT, SURVIVOR OF THE RACE OF WINGED LIZARDS, HOVERS IN THE AIR, HIGH OVER THE HERD.

IT CROSSES OVER THE REGION, OBEYING AN ARCANE INSTINCT, FAR FROM THE SEA WHERE IT NORMALLY LIVES.

IT SURVEYS THE VAST NORTH: BROAD PLAINS WHITE WITH FROST, SHADOWY FORESTS, AND, ON THE HORIZON, MOUNTAINS WHERE THE ICE NEVER MELTS. ITS ROUTES HAVE CHANGED, PERHAPS BECAUSE THE WORLD ITSELF IS CHANGING, IN THIS ERA OF THE LAST DINOSAURS.

THE CONTINENTS ARE MOVING, THE EASTERN LANDS BREAKING UP AND SPITTING FIRE, LIKE INFECTED WOUNDS.

A NEW SEA CAUSES NEW SEASONS TO ARISE IN THE DINOSAURS' DOMAIN . . .

. . . OVER WHOSE GRANDEUR THERE FLUTTERS A VAGUE AND PALLID FEELING OF DECLINE.

BACK ON THE GROUND . . .

. . . AN AMAZING CREATURE IS POKING ITS STRONG BUT SENSITIVE BEAK IN THE SNOW, NOSING FOR FOOD. KIN OF THE SHIELD-BEARERS, THIS THREE-HORNED BEAST HAS A SHIELD, TOO. BRAVE, IRRITABLE, AND SOLITARY, HIS KIND VIES FOR MASTERY OF THE NORTH.

HE IS ANCIENT; HIS SHIELD AND SNOUT BEAR SCARS OF BATTLES WITH RIVALS AND HUNTERS.

HE LOST HIS LEFT EYE WHEN A WOUND BECAME INFECTED.

CREAK

HE CLEARS SNOW, SHIFTS A FALLEN TREE . . .

THROW

. . . UNTIL HE LOCATES A YOUNG SHRUB.

HE EATS AVIDLY.

THE SILENCE HERE IS ABSOLUTE.

SOMETHING IS NOT RIGHT.

HE STOPS FORAGING TO LISTEN.

WAS THAT THE SHADOW OF A NOISE, ADDED TO THE SOFT MURMURING OF AIR AMONG THE BRANCHES?

NO. SILENCE.

THE OLD BEAST TURNS HIS HEAD, LOOKING. BUT HIS WEAK SIGHT IS MADE EVEN WORSE BECAUSE HE HAS ONLY ONE EYE.

HE RESUMES HIS MEAL.

SILENCE.

AND YET SOMETHING IS THERE, IN THE WOODS. THE WARRIOR HALTS AGAIN.

THE CARNIVORE TEARS
IN AGAIN, BUT—
WHO KNOWS HOW—
HIS PREY BREAKS FREE.

HIS
WOUNDS ARE
TERRIBLE.

THE TWO HUGE
FIGHTERS PANT, GASPING
FOR AIR, SNORTING
MOISTURE FROM
WIDE-OPEN
MOUTHS,

STUDYING
EACH OTHER.

IN FACT, THE THREE-HORNED
ONE IS TRYING TO TURN AND
ATTACK, BUT HIS WOUNDS LIMIT
HIS MOVEMENTS.

PANT

PANT

PANT

PANT

THE KING'S
MOVES HAVE
PURPOSE . . .

HE KEEPS ON HIS PREY'S BLIND SIDE AND
THUS HAS THE UPPER HAND.

THE VEGETARIAN
CHARGES . . .

. . . BUT
STUMBLES.

AN APPARENTLY MERCILESS DRAMA.

THE TYRANT POUNCES AGAIN ON HIS FOE.

HE GRABS THE VITAL SPOT, THE NECK, WHICH THE TIRED OLD WARRIOR HAS LEFT EXPOSED.

HE BITES WITH HIS BODY'S ENTIRE FORCE, TEARING.

THE KING'S CONCENTRATED POWER IS ENOUGH TO PROVOKE ONE MORE DESPERATE RALLY.

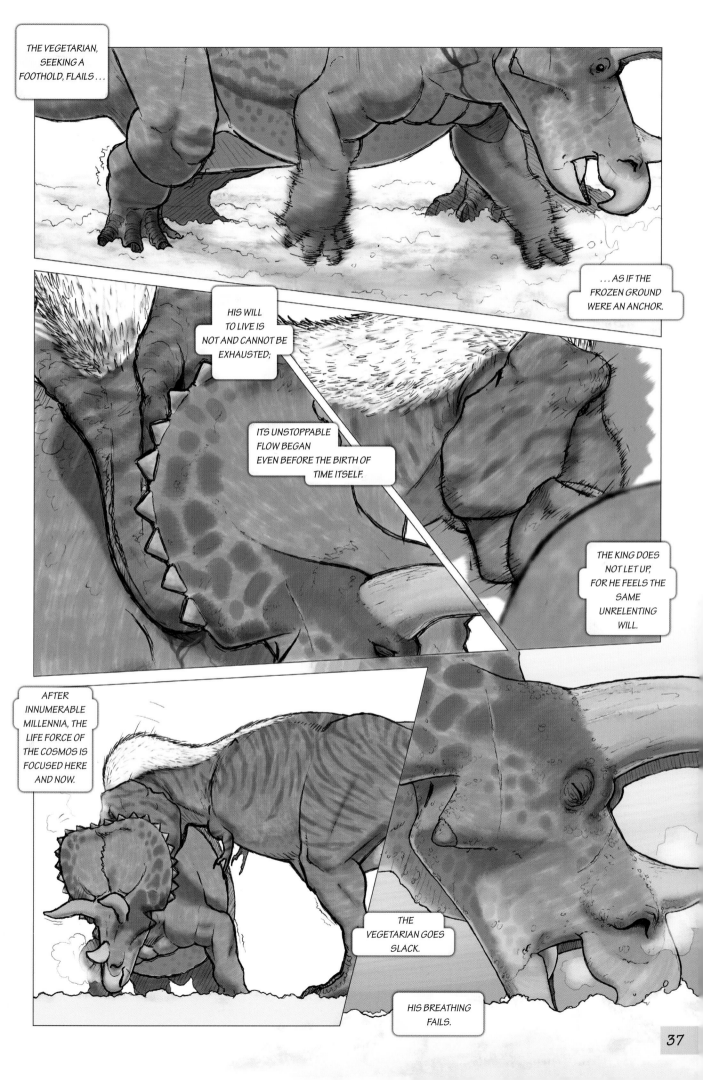

IT IS ONLY LIFE FROM DEATH, CHANGE IN STASIS.

NATURE CREATES ALL, CHANGES ALL, AND DESTROYS NOTHING. IT IS EVERYTHING AND NEVER FINISHED, ETERNALLY EVOLVING.

THERE IS NO EXPLANATION FOR HUMANS AS THEY CONSIDER THE END OF THE LIFE OF A SINGLE CREATURE OR THAT OF AN ENTIRE POWERFUL RACE.

NATURE DOES NOT CLARIFY. IT EXISTS.

EONS AND INNUMERABLE EXISTENCES ARE AN INFINITE FLOW THAT HAS NO BEGINNING AND THEREFORE NO END.

ALL IS ONLY THE ETERNAL HERE AND NOW.

DINOSAUR EVOLUTION

This diagram of the evolution of the dinosaurs (in which the red lines represent evolutionary branches for which there is fossil evidence) shows the two principal groups (the saurischians and ornithischians) and their evolutionary path through time during the Mesozoic. Among the saurischians (to the right), we can see the evolution of the sauropodomorphs, who were all herbivores and were the largest animals ever to walk the earth. Farther to the right, still among the saurischians, we find the theropods. Among the theropods there quite soon emerges a line characterized by rigid tails (Tetanurae), from which, through the maniraptors, birds (Aves) evolve. The ornithischians (to the left), which were all herbivores, have an equally complicated evolutionary history, which begins with the basic *Pisanosaurus* type but soon splits into Thyreophora ("shield bearers," such as ankylosaurs and stegosaurs) on the one hand, and Genasauria ("lizards with cheeks") on the other. The latter in turn evolve into two principal lines: the marginocephalians, which include ceratopsians, and euornithopods, which include the most flourishing herbivores of the Mesozoic, the hadrosaurs.

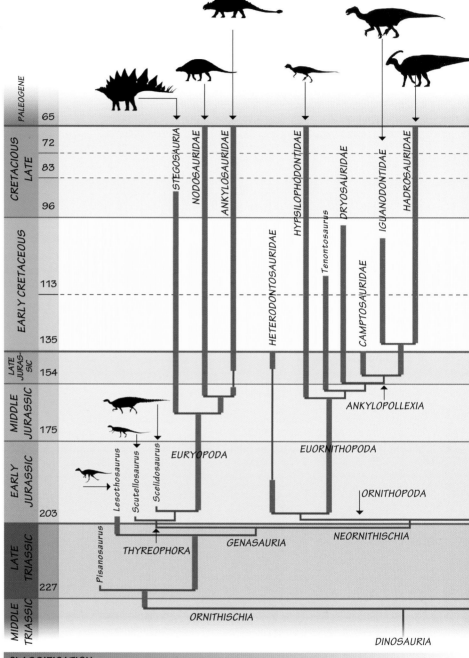

	PALEOGENE	65
CRETACIOUS	LATE	72
		83
		96
	EARLY CRETACEOUS	113
		135
	LATE JURASSIC	154
	MIDDLE JURASSIC	175
	EARLY JURASSIC	203
	LATE TRIASSIC	227
	MIDDLE TRIASSIC	

STEGOSAURIA · NODOSAURIDAE · ANKYLOSAURIDAE · HETERODONTOSAURIDAE · HYPSILOPHODONTIDAE · *Tenontosaurus* · DRYOSAURIDAE · CAMPTOSAURIDAE · IGUANODONTIDAE · HADROSAURIDAE

ANKYLOPOLLEXIA
EURYOPODA
EUORNITHOPODA
ORNITHOPODA

Lesothosaurus · *Scutellosaurus* · *Scelidosaurus* · *Pisanosaurus*

THYREOPHORA · GENASAURIA · NEORNITHISCHIA

ORNITHISCHIA

DINOSAURIA

IDENTIKIT *(see page 8)*

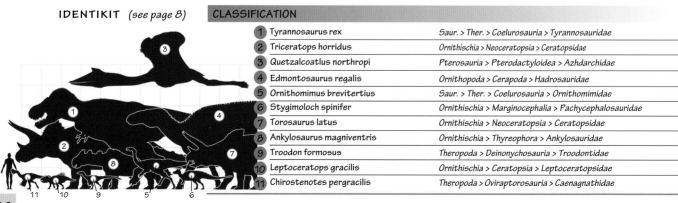

CLASSIFICATION

1	Tyrannosaurus rex	*Saur. > Ther. > Coelurosauria > Tyrannosauridae*
2	Triceratops horridus	*Ornithischia > Neoceratopsia > Ceratopsidae*
3	Quetzalcoatlus northropi	*Pterosauria > Pterodactyloidea > Azhdarchidae*
4	Edmontosaurus regalis	*Ornithopoda > Cerapoda > Hadrosauridae*
5	Ornithomimus brevitertius	*Saur. > Ther. > Coelurosauria > Ornithomimidae*
6	Stygimoloch spinifer	*Ornithischia > Marginocephalia > Pachycephalosauridae*
7	Torosaurus latus	*Ornithischia > Neoceratopsia > Ceratopsidae*
8	Ankylosaurus magniventris	*Ornithischia > Thyreophora > Ankylosauridae*
9	Troodon formosus	*Theropoda > Deinonychosauria > Troodontidae*
10	Leptoceratops gracilis	*Ornithischia > Ceratopsia > Leptoceratopsidae*
11	Chirostenotes pergracilis	*Theropoda > Oviraptorosauria > Caenagnathidae*

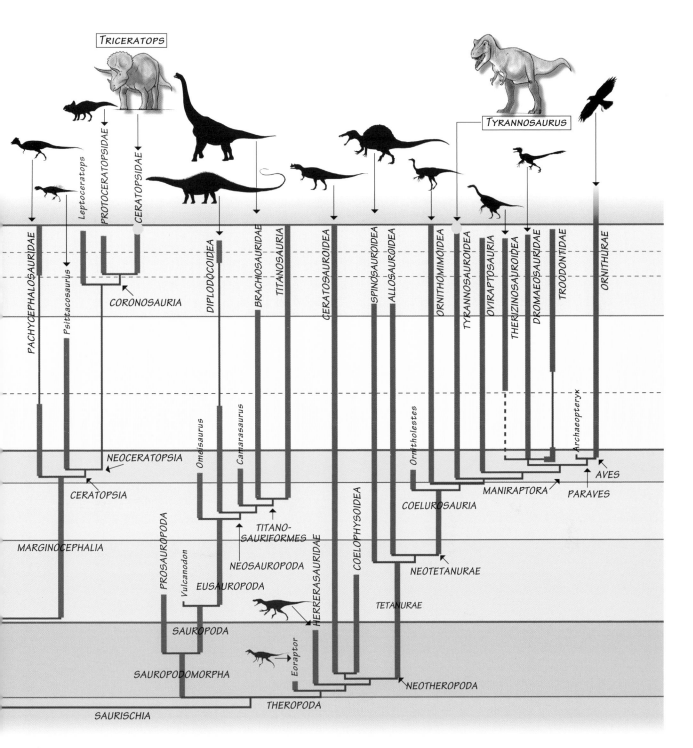

TRICERATOPS

TYRANNOSAURUS

PACHYCEPHALOSAURIDAE
Psittacosaurus
Leptoceratops
PROTOCERATOPSIDAE
CERATOPSIDAE
DIPLODOCOIDEA
BRACHIOSAURIDAE
TITANOSAURIA
CERATOSAUROIDEA
SPINOSAUROIDEA
ALLOSAUROIDEA
ORNITHOMIMOIDEA
TYRANNOSAUROIDEA
OVIRAPTOSAURIA
THERIZINOSAUROIDEA
DROMAEOSAURIDAE
TROODONTIDAE
ORNITHURAE

CORONOSAURIA

Omeisaurus
Camarasaurus
Ornitholestes
Archaeopteryx

AVES

NEOCERATOPSIA
MANIRAPTORA
PARAVES

CERATOPSIA
COELUROSAURIA

TITANO-
SAURIFORMES

NEOSAUROPODA
NEOTETANURAE

PROSAUROPODA
Vulcanodon
HERRERASAURIDAE
COELOPHYSOIDEA

EUSAUROPODA
TETANURAE

MARGINOCEPHALIA

SAUROPODA

Eoraptor

SAUROPODOMORPHA
NEOTHEROPODA

THEROPODA

SAURISCHIA

LENGTH	HEIGHT	WEIGHT	DIET	PERIOD		TERRITORY
over 39 feet	over 13 feet	over 5 tons	meat	Late Cretaceous (Maastrichtian)		North America
over 29 feet	over 9 feet	up to 10 tons	plants	Late Cretaceous (Maastrichtian)		North America
wingspan: 46 feet		unknown	fish	Late Cretaceous (Campanian–Maastrichtian)		North America
over 42 feet	over 13 feet	over 5 tons	plants	Late Cretaceous (Maastrichtian)		North America
over 11 feet	6.5 feet	over 660 pounds	omnivorous	Late Cretaceous (Campanian–Maastrichtian)		North America
up to 9.75 feet	approx. 3 feet	up to 880 pounds	plants	Late Cretaceous (Maastrichtian)		North America
over 23 feet	over 8 feet	up to 6 tons	plants	Late Cretaceous (Maastrichtian)		North America
up to 29.5 feet	over 6.5 feet	over 7 tons	plants	Late Cretaceous (Maastrichtian)		North America
over 6.5 feet	approx. 3 feet	up to 110 pounds	meat	Late Cretaceous (Campanian–Maastrichtian)		North America
up to 6 feet	over 19 inches	up to 400 pounds	plants	Late Cretaceous (Maastrichtian)		North America
up to 6.5 feet	approx. 3 feet	over 110 pounds	plants	Late Cretaceous (Campanian–Maastrichtian)		North America

THE CRETACEOUS
THE TWILIGHT OF THE GODS

▲ An overall view of the Canadian badlands on an October morning. The temperature range in this region is unusually wide: from 30°F at 8:00 in the morning to more than 64°F at noon. In the photo you can clearly see the geological strata. Dinosaur remains are quite common throughout, while the top layers originated in a marine environment.

▲ The sign that indicates the beginning of the "tourist" path through the badlands.

The North American Badlands

The dinosaur era came to a glorious end, consumed perhaps in the flames of colossal volcanic eruptions or perhaps in the lethal light of a meteor impact or two. But before discussing that end—and before discovering that it was not really an end—it is worthwhile to take a final look at the end of the reign of the "terrible lizards."

The Late Cretaceous in North America witnessed the most famous dinosaurs of all, animals that have become veritable icons, even for those who are not fans of paleontology. Names such as *Tyrannosaurus* and *Triceratops* are known to practically everyone, and those who have read any book at all on dinosaurs will recall *Ankylosaurus*,

Ornithomimus, and perhaps even *Torosaurus*. Moreover, the media have glorified many of the animals discovered in the layers of the Late Cretaceous. Again, just think of *Tyrannosaurus*, which has become synonymous with *Jurassic Park*, but also with the whole idea of what is enormous and dangerous.

And so let's take a look at the time when our story unfolds, when the planet was at the end of perhaps its most epic era. The world of the Late Cretaceous, as we shall soon see, was very similar to that of today. There would have been many animals similar to those of the modern world, but dinosaurs still ruled the earth. Their forms were as varied as ever, and their size was still considerable, although they no longer approached the records of the titans of the past. One of the best places to look for Late Cretaceous dinosaurs is North America, in an area that now straddles Canada and the United States; in fact, our story takes place in present-day Canada. Since the early twentieth century, finds have been made in this region, often called the "badlands" due to both their physical and their climatic conditions. This area, parched by the sun and cleaved by frost, traversed by more or less impressive rivers, is a veritable dinosaur cemetery. Much of the badlands was created from sediments that accumu-

lated along enormous river valleys or near the sea; this was the perfect environment for fossilizing the bones of giant dinosaurs but a bit less suitable for preserving the skeletons of smaller animals. Nevertheless, dinosaur paleontology came of age here, where generations of famous scientists took turns extracting from the badlands the bones of creatures that seem to have emerged from legend. The most famous is probably *Tyrannosaurus rex*, the only animal that has the privilege of being called by its exact name: *T. rex*. *Tyrannosaurus* is the name of the genus, while *Tyrannosaurus rex* is that of the species. (The lowercase name *rex* is what scientists call the "trivial name.") The epitome of dinosaurs, the dinosaur par excellence, *Tyrannosaurus* has occupied a massive place in popular culture, appearing in films ever since the dawn of cinema, as well as comic strips and literary tales, even becoming the name of a rock band—although *Deinonychus* also has that honor.

Leaving the U.S. border behind us, let's follow the tracks of the ancient lords of the planet into Canada, more or less to the center of North

America: a vast, almost infinite plain, strewn with enormous wheat fields. The sun is setting, and the horizon is so endless that you can already see the moon, across the sky. The plain extends as far as the eye can see, until it touches the sky beyond the cultivated fields. And then the first low, barren hills appear, the vegetation becomes increasingly sparse, and the badlands begin. The name undoubtedly evokes a territory that is not exactly pleasant, and in fact for those who find themselves in this strange place for the first time, the badlands really seem almost to be cursed: barren earth, they have very little vegetation, and the temperature can vary by more than 30°F over the course of the day. And yet for a dinosaur lover this is one of the most perfect places on earth. You cannot take a step without coming across some clue, some element of the past; the discovery of invertebrate or vertebrate remains is practically the norm here. The badlands are the result of the erosion of sedimentary layers of different types, those of continental origin lying beneath marine accumulations.

Perhaps one of the most spectacular places to observe this is near Drumheller, Canada. This small city was literally founded on the gifts of the subsoil. Built as a coal station, it became one of the most famous places for dinosaur lovers and scholars, in part thanks to the impressive local museum, the Royal Tyrrell Museum of Palaeontology, which boasts what is probably the largest collection of fossils in Canada. The museum is set directly atop the badlands, and many almost complete skeletons have been discovered just a few dozen yards away from the exhibition halls. And it is in environments such as this that traces of gigantic river valleys, like the one in which our story takes place, have been discovered. If it were possible to go back in time, and if we were to stand at the site of the entrance to the Tyrrell Museum, we would find ourselves in a gigantic valley rich in alluvial deposits, where we could witness the scenes from our story narrated by the sun at the close of the dinosaur era. Just imagine the last giants at their height here, soon to end their saga in a final explosion of glory, never again to adorn our world.

In the long winter the badlands are blanketed in white; the snow is frequently abundant and the temperatures extremely severe. It must have been this way at the time of the dinosaurs as well, and our story takes place during one such snowy season close to the Arctic Circle. Not much is known about dinosaurs' adaptations to the cold; we can guess that some of them changed location, making seasonal migrations, while others stayed put and sought to feed themselves and fight for their lives, a bit like what goes on in this same territory today among wolves, bears, caribou, and arctic hares. We know that some dinosaurs had very large eye sockets, and this could be a sign that their visual capacity had adapted to the dim light of long winters, but unfortunately most adaptations to the cold—at least in modern animals—are metabolic in origin or in any case detectable only in the soft tissue missing from most dinosaur fossils. Thus, we can only imagine that dinosaurs behaved a bit like today's large mammals in the way they dealt with the cold and the snow.

▲ The entrance to the Royal Tyrrell Museum of Palaeontology, located in the badlands, near the small town of Drumheller (Alberta, Canada).

Once a mining center and then a penal colony, today Drumheller is a favorite destination for dinosaur lovers.

Dinosaurs of the Late Cretaceous in North America

During the final period of the dinosaur era, North America was a region of vast plains, traversed by rivers, that skirted the epicontinental seas. Many, many dinosaurs passed through these plains, and it is no accident that those who are interested in dinosaur paleontology often find themselves thinking about the deserts of North America. In fact, this is where the most famous giants of the past have been discovered.

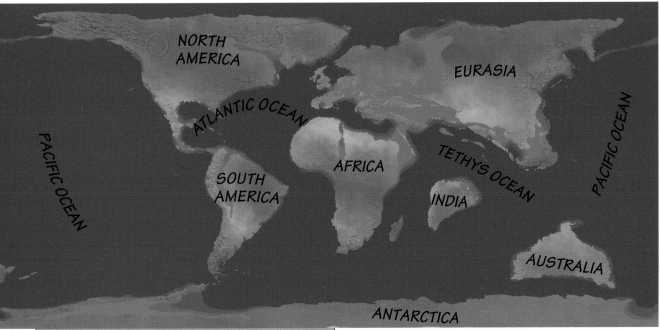

▲ Top: the appearance of our planet at the end of the Cretaceous. The continents have nearly assumed their present-day configurations (see inset), except for India, which is journeying toward a collision with Eurasia. Australia has long been adrift, and in fact its fauna will still have unique characteristics in our time. The red circle shows the location of our story.

▶ Stratigraphic division of the Cretaceous. The final stage of the Late Cretaceous, the Maastrichtian (during which our story takes place), gets its name from the Dutch city of Maastricht, where sedimentary marine rocks are found. Maastricht played a small but famous role in the history of paleontology, when Napoleon Bonaparte ordered that the skeleton of a mosasaur discovered there be claimed for France, in exchange for some barrels of wine.

CRETACEOUS	UPPER OR LATE CRETACEOUS	Maastrichtian	72–65 million years ago
		Campanian	83–72 million years ago
		Santonian	87–83 million years ago
		Coniacian	88–87 (85?) million years ago
		Turonian	92–88 million years ago
		Cenomanian	96–92 million years ago
	LOWER OR EARLY CRETACEOUS	Albian	108–96 million years ago
		Aptian	113–108 million years ago
		Barremian	117–113 million years ago
		Hauterivian	123–117 million years ago
		Valanginian	131–123 million years ago
		Berriasian	135–131 million years ago

Theropods

The protagonist of our story is *Tyrannosaurus* **∗1**. The name of this gigantic carnivore means "reptile tyrant," and its species name, *rex*, translates as "king." In 1905, when the great paleontologist Henry Fairfield Osborn described the remains of this magnificent creature, he gave it the most magniloquent name possible, to clarify beyond any shadow of a doubt that it would never have any equal on Earth, that it was indeed "king" of the dinosaurs. His reasoning is easy to understand; this colossal predator, equipped with tiny forelimbs, each of which had only two fingers **∗2**, very closely recalls a shark with feet. Its rear limbs were quite stocky, and while it is almost impossible to precisely estimate the speed of dinosaurs, we can assume that the thrust its muscles could provide was considerable **∗3**! But the most astounding part of a *T. rex* skeleton is undoubtedly the skull. A *Tyrannosaurus* skull is simply gigantic, built to devastate. The teeth, which can be up to 6 inches long, are pointed and sharp, and the deep jaws were clearly quite powerful **∗4**. From time to time, certain paleontologists—principally Jack Horner and his students—have declared an extremely personal war against the "reptile tyrant," maintaining that this colossal predator was actually an overgrown

▶ *One of the authors (Matteo Bacchin) in front of a* Tyrannosaurus *skeleton. From this angle we can appreciate the massive head, which must have been this gigantic carnivore's principal weapon. The hind legs are clearly built to provide the animal's body with a powerful thrust.*

∗1
page 15
panel 4

∗2
page 15
panel 4

∗3
page 31
panel 2

∗4
page 21
panel 4

vulture, and that it fed exclusively off dead animals, being too slow and weak to hunt. But these hypotheses serve only to gain their promoters a moment of notoriety in sensationalist headlines, since we have evidence of *Tyrannosaurus* attacks on animals that survived their bites. In fact, we have proof that tyrannosaurs actively hunted, not to mention that—apart from vultures—no tetrapod has been exclusively necrophagous (carrion-eating). However, as I often like to say, no one would turn down a free hamburger, and *Tyrannosaurus* would have almost certainly eaten a carcass when it found one: free food is free food, after all ✳5! *Tyrannosaurus* has been found in the United States and Canada, and in Canada there are other, slightly smaller tyrannosaurids, such as *Albertosaurus* and *Gorgosaurus*. All share the small didactylous arms and the shape and structure of the skull. But scholars have recently discovered that the early tyrannosaurs were less massive and more similar to other carnivores. *Di long*, discovered in China a short time ago, demonstrates that small, primitive tyrannosaurs were probably covered with feathers, while another fascinating find from late 2009, *Proceratosaurus*, has provided an unusual image of the early tyrannosaur as a not very large animal, with a strange and yet-to-be-explained horn on its snout. "Standard" tyrannosaurs, however, have also been discovered outside North America, and the most famous is undoubtedly *Tarbosaurus*, which in the past was also identified as *Tyrannosaurus* and, for a brief period, known as *Jenghizkhan*, after Genghis Khan.

In the plains of the Late Cretaceous, *Tyrannosaurus* may have been the largest carnivore, but it certainly was not the only one. In our story there are three other theropods, two of which were in all likelihood omnivores or even herbivores. Let's begin by looking closely at the smallest predator in our story. Its name is *Troodon*, or "tooth that wounds," because the first find of this small carnivore consisted of some serrated teeth. Later fossils made it possible to compile a complete picture of *Troodon* ✳6, and some interesting discoveries have been made. For example, according to some scholars the first finger of its front limbs might have been partially opposable to the other two ✳7. The eye sockets are very large, and it is possible

that *Troodon* had certain adaptations enabling it to be a nocturnal predator; perhaps it hunted mammals in the dark. There has been much speculation about the volume of its brain, to the point that, in the 1980s, the paleontologist Dale Russell conceived and constructed a model of a "dinosauroid," a creature that could have later developed from *Troodon*, if it evolved in a manner similar to our own. Curiously, after this strange statue appeared in museums and books, a popular myth about reptile aliens emerged . . . but that is another story. The small *Troodon* also had another interesting characteristic: as in dromeosaurs, in troodontids the claw of the second toe of the foot is more developed than the other toes, and it was probably used like those of present-day **ratites**,

▲ *Tyrannosaurus. The impressive depth of the lower jaw gave this predator one of the most powerful bites in nature. The pressure of its jaws enabled its sharp teeth to cut through muscles, tendons, and bones.*

▲ *Detail of the hind foot, in which it is possible to see a very distinctive bony structure: the central foot bone, or meta-tarsal, is "compressed" by the two lateral metatarsals. This condition, known as "arctometatarsal," makes it possible to classify* Tyrannosaurus *and its relatives in a different group from other carnosaurs.*

✳5
page 25
panel 3

✳6
page 24
panel 3

✳7
page 24
panel 3

for kicking possible aggressors. A modern ostrich can easily kill a man with a kick, and so it may be that *Troodon* was well equipped to defend itself.

The other two theropods in our story are truly remarkable. The first is *Ornithomimus* ✱**8**. It was named the "bird mimic" by Charles Othniel Marsh in 1890, because the skeleton of this graceful theropod recalls that of an ostrich. We have already encountered ornithomimids such as *Pelecanimimus* in our stories, and the general shape of this group always remains the same: long neck, small head, long arms, and relatively weak wrists. In effect, *Ornithomimus* would have been just like an ostrich with a tail. As we have already hinted, paleontologists still do not agree about the diet of these animals. While they were toothless and, as far as we can tell, equipped with plates in their beaks ✱**9**, we still don't fully understand what they lived on, but it is generally thought that they were omnivorous. *Ornithomimus* probably lived in large groups to avoid both the small and large predators of the era. The other unusual theropod in our story is *Chirostenotes* ✱**10**, whose name means "narrow hand." One of the curious things about this animal is that it was discovered and described in pieces—first the hands (*Chirostenotes*), then the feet (*Macrophalangia*), and finally the jaws (*Caenagnathus*). Then researchers realized that these three animals were in fact parts of the same one! This type of "error" is very common in paleontology, as we have seen. Today we know that *Chirostenotes* was an oviraptorid—a relative of the more famous *Oviraptor*. It is yet another bizarre theropod about whose diet we still know practically nothing.

▲ *A more up-to-date conception of a dinosauroid than that seen in the statue created by Dale Russell and Ron Seguin in the 1980s. However interesting this evolutionary hypothesis is, it is highly unlikely that a theropod could have evolved into a form so similar to mammal primates.*

▼ *This Citipati, an oviraptorid of the Late Cretaceous, was discovered crouching on its eggs, protecting them with the plumage of its arms.*

▼ *An oviraptorid skull. Every member of this group, related to Chirostenotes, has a different skull, but they are all characterized by a short and massive beak, a lack of teeth, and a crest on the top of the skull. All the known skulls are full of perforations that probably served to lighten the structure.*

✱**8**
page 17 panel 1

✱**9**
page 17 panel 3

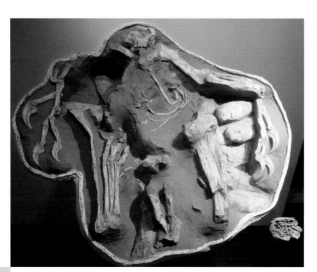

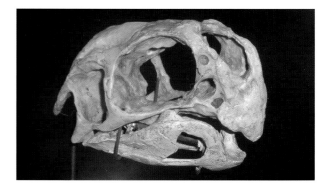

Ornithischians

As in the modern era, in the dinosaur era there were a greater number and variety of herbivores than carnivores. Many researchers have considered this similarity between the fauna of the two eras as indirect proof of the fact that dinosaurs were homeotherms (warm-blooded). We do not have the tools to make a comparison, but since we now know about the homeothermy of dinosaurs thanks to other, previously discussed evidence, the resemblance between the fauna of the two eras could be much more than a coincidence. Thus, in the Late Cretaceous in North America we find many ornithischians, all extremely interesting and strange, some of which have become well-known stars among dinosaur fans. Let's begin with the "oldest" in terms of origins. The U.S. news media recently reported the discovery of a new armored dinosaur, calling it "the Sherman tank of dinosaurs." This seems ludicrous to both paleontologists and weapons experts, since the Sherman was one of the worst armored tanks in history. Ankylosaurs were animals with impressive armor, and a more accurate comparison would be to the German PzKpfw VI, better known as the "Tiger," or to the Soviet T-34. *Ankylosaurus* **✳11**, the dinosaur that gives the group its name, was, indeed, a living tank. The bony armor it wore was extremely thick, in some cases up to 4 inches, and it was absolutely

▲ An Ankylosaurus *head. Note the total absence of openings (except, obviously, the nose and eyes). In reality the skull of* Ankylosaurus *has the same openings as all other dinosaurs, but they are covered with bony plates, making the defense of this moving fortress absolutely complete and impenetrable.*

impervious to any predators lacking antitank missiles **✳12**! Like its relatives, *Ankylosaurus* did not rely only on passive defenses, but also had a bony thickening at the tip of its tail (as we saw in our fourth story), similar to the reinforced club of a medieval knight **✳13**. And so *Ankylosaurus* was free to walk about—very slowly—through the plains of the Cretaceous, practically ignoring the predators there. But like present-day tanks, it would have had to avoid soft or waterlogged terrain. Because of its primitive teeth, its plant-based diet would not have been particularly refined.

Unlike *Ankylosaurus*, the two groups we can truly call the rulers of the Late Cretaceous exhibit considerable evolution of their jaws and teeth, as we have seen in the previous volumes. These

✳10
page 19
panel 3

✳11
page 26
panel 5

✳12
page 26
panel 5

✳13
page 26
panel 6

▲ *Hadrosaurs belonging to the subfamily of hadrosaurines, such as* Edmontosaurus, *did not have crests, but they did have enormous and well-developed nasal passages; this led to the hypothesis that hadrosaurines had "inflatable" pockets, a bit like present-day frogs, that they used to communicate with their fellow creatures. (photo: Ballista, Wikimedia)*

A famous Edmontosaurus mummy. In these mummies, we can see the skin, some internal structures such as muscles and tendons, and even, in a recently discovered example, possibly the tongue and what is probably subcutaneous fat.

are the Hadrosauridae, on the one hand, and the Marginocephalia, on the other.

Hadrosaurs were probably the most widespread dinosaurs in the world; they were large herbivores (in the previous volumes we saw that they also "invented" chewing), and paleontologists divide them into two groups, depending on whether they have complex nasal passages and crests (Lambeosaurinae) or no crests (Hadrosaurinae). In our story, we encounter a hadrosaur called *Edmontosaurus* ✳14, whose structure is typical of this group: massive, quadrupedal (but probably also able to walk on two feet), and equipped with a curious ducklike bill and broad nasal chambers ✳15. This animal is very well known because not only its bones but also true fossil mummies have been discovered; from these, specialists have been able to extract extremely important data regarding everything from the nervous system to the digestive apparatus, muscles, and skin. *Edmontosaurus* was an herbivore capable of chewing, and it was considerable in size, up to 43 feet in length. Some paleontologists are convinced that *Anatotitan*, or "duck titan," the largest of the

hadrosaurs, is the same genus as *Edmontosaurus*. Hadrosaurs were able to reproduce very effectively, and they could eat almost any plant. For this reason, they, along with the ceratopsians, which we shall soon get to, were the true "everyman" of the Late Cretaceous and the most widely disseminated animals on the planet at that time. However, as far as we know, *Edmontosaurus* had just one form of defense: the group. This enormous animal possessed neither passive nor active deterrents to attack, and we can imagine it as being like a gigantic cow on the grassy plains of the Cretaceous.

The Marginocephalia, however, were able to turn one of their trademarks into a defensive element, although they were not as specialized as ankylosaurs or stegosaurs. In this group there are two large evolutionary lines, the Pachycephalosauridae ("heavy-headed reptiles") and the Ceratopsia ("horned faces"). In our story, *Stygimoloch* ✳16 ("demon of the Styx"; Moloch is a deity associated with fire in many Mideastern religions) represents the first group. This small dinosaur had a body typical of ornithischian

◄ Triceratops, one of the largest and potentially most dangerous herbivores of the Cretaceous. (photo: V. Santaniello)

▶ Two dueling Stegoceras. There is no conclusive evidence of head-butting duels between pachycephalosaurs. We do know that their bone structure reveals a strengthening of the skull and the spinal column, but some paleontologists caution against imagining them like modern goats. Clearly, the massive skull, reinforced and adorned with horns, must have evolved for an activity that was not exactly peaceful, but perhaps it was as a defense against predators.

bipeds, but its head, its "strong point," was almost completely covered in spikes and plates, making it both a defensive and an offensive weapon ✳17. We do not know exactly how the pachycephalosaurs used this armed head, but the group's wide range and evolution attest to the excellence of the design. However, the structure of pachycephalosaurs is not only intriguing but also conservative, meaning that in the various genera, the postcranial skeletons closely resemble one another, so much so that Horner and his group have hypothesized that *Stygimoloch* was only a youthful form of the larger *Pachycephalosaurus*. As we shall see shortly, this is not the only osteological hypothesis that could lead to confusion in the world of dinosaur paleontologists.

The other group of Marginocephalia is the Ceratopsia. *Leptoceratops* ✳18 ("small horned face"), the small biped in our story, belongs to a group of ceratopsians that includes only a few genera, all of which were limited in size and probably swift in their movements. Like their larger cousins, animals such as the *Leptoceratops* also had parrotlike, toothless beaks and bony ruffs ✳19. *Leptoceratops* was a small herbivore that probably wasn't even troubled by large predators, but smaller animals such as *Troodon* possibly preyed on it. Yet it was its large cousins that literally caused North America to tremble. *Triceratops* ✳20 ("three-horned face"), one of the most famous dinosaurs, was a colossus, equipped with a small bony ruff and three horns, two long ones over its eyes and one shorter one on its nose. It was a quadrupedal herbivore, capable of eating many types of plants,

which it cut into pieces with its parrotlike beak and then chewed with its powerful sets of teeth. Normally we imagine it as a very irascible type of rhinoceros. Certainly it was very formidable when angry. We have evidence that *Triceratops* was attacked by *Tyrannosaurus*, and for decades the struggle between the two creatures has been an icon of dinosaur art. Yet despite its size, *Triceratops* probably was not the most dangerous in its group, because its bony ruff was rather small. Among the ceratopsians with a longer ruff (in our fourth story we saw an example of how they could defend themselves), *Torosaurus* ✳21 was undoubtedly the oddest. Its name does not mean "bull reptile," as many believe, but rather "perforated reptile," because its very long, bony ruff had two enormous holes. *Torosaurus* also had three horns, and its skull resembled that of *Triceratops*. In fact, as recently as September 2009 Horner's circle (in a series of valuable osteological studies) maintained that *Torosaurus* is in reality a mature *Triceratops*. For now that hypothesis has not been confirmed, but in paleontology everything is possible.

✳14
page 23
panel 3

✳16
page 21
panel 1

✳15
page 23
panel 4

✳17
page 21
panel 3

✳18
page 18
panel 4

✳19
page 18
panel 5

✳20
page 29
panel 2

✳21
page 27
panel 2

MB'10

Other Animals

As mentioned earlier, Late Cretaceous fauna in North America did not consist exclusively of dinosaurs. Despite the very great evolutionary success of avian theropods (birds) *22, pterosaurs continued to exist, with a clear tendency to increase in size, probably precisely in order to compete with the new flying creatures. North America was the first place where the remains of gigantic pterosaurs were discovered, such as *Pteranodon*, whose wingspan could reach 26 feet.

However, one of the largest pterosaurs was undoubtedly the one we encounter in our story: *Quetzalcoatlus* *23. Its name comes from that of an Aztec deity, Quetzalcoatl, the "plumed serpent." Despite the fact that it is the most famous representative of the Azhdarchidae, a family of pterosaurs known for their great size, we still know relatively little about *Quetzalcoatlus*. Because of the nature of pterosaur bones (hollow, fragile, and **trabeculated**), the fossil remains that have been attributed to this animal with certainty are, in fact, relatively few in number and poorly preserved. We know that it could have had a wingspan of up to approximately 39, or even 46, feet—no small dimension—and we know that it was toothless and had a long neck. In the 1980s it was hypothesized that *Quetzalcoatlus* was a vulture-pterosaur that whirled above the alluvial plains in search of carcasses to eat. This hypothesis no longer finds much support today, and it is thought that the "plumed serpent"—which, for the record, was not related to snakes and had no feathers—was in fact principally a fish eater.

Toward the end of the Cretaceous, because of the merciless competition from their rivals, pterosaurs

▲ *Pteranodon sternbergi*. Their wingspan could exceed 23 feet, and it is thought that these enormous creatures may have flown as much as 600 to 900 miles from the coast, spending much of their lives in the air, like the modern albatross. We still have no valid explanation for the bizarre crests of pterosaurs.

▼ A forelimb of Quetzalcoatlus. Although known only from fragmentary remains, this is surely one of the largest flying animals in history, perhaps the largest. Its remains have also been discovered far from water, although we do not know how much time it spent away from the coast.

*22
page 14
panel 3

*23
page 28
panel 1/2

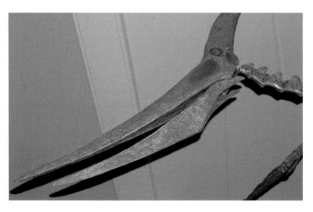

▲ Detail of the skull of *Pteranodon longiceps*. The elongated crest and the deep lower jaw are clearly visible. The discovery of the remains of fish positioned immediately beneath the lower jaw has led some to think it had a throat sac, a bit like the one found in modern pelicans.

attained adaptive solutions that pushed the limits of engineering: incredible dimensions, structures that seem to come from mythological tales, and perhaps a quest for environments less colonized by birds. While their competitors, equipped with feathers and teeth, hunted along the shore, the great flying pterosaurs roamed farther and farther out, challenging winds and currents, venturing hundreds of miles from the coast, a long way from the most distant sites that birds could reach. Certain pterosaurs evolved toward other eating strategies—for obtaining fruit, insects, and perhaps other animals—while birds rapidly colonized one ecological niche after another. In the Cretaceous there were already nonflying birds, similar to ostriches and probably related to them, that were capable of living on dry land, while *Ichthyornis*, similar to gulls with teeth, patrolled the skies, and *Hesperornis* were able to plunge deep into the water, skillfully maneuvering in the seas to hunt fish and flee from hungry jaws.

The seas were withdrawing from higher lands, yet marine fauna flourished more than ever. Ichthyosaurs had now vanished from the seas, but the last plesiosaurs, creatures with extremely elongated necks, sought desperately to stay competitive with the new, lethal predators: lizards perfectly adapted to marine life called mosasaurs. These were colossal in size, armed with pointed teeth and powerful jaws capable of breaking bones and shells with equal ease. Sharks, after an uncertain period, gave rise to the most lethal predatory machines to ever live: neoselachians, with forms very similar to present-day great white sharks. These ferocious predators could also feed off carcasses if need be, as is shown by the discovery of certain dinosaur bones that bear the obvious signs of shark teeth.

Nor was life simple in the continental waters; gigantic crocodiles lay in ambush for dinosaurs in the low waters of the swamps, as we saw in our fifth book, and huge tortoises warmed themselves in the Cretaceous sun.

Mammals also became quite widespread, and these were not the small, uncertain animals of an earlier time, but genuine mammals capable of giving birth to and nursing offspring *24. Based on the specific morphology of certain moths, some scholars have hypothesized that bats had already evolved in the Late Cretaceous. Their reasoning is that moths whose fossils they have studied seem to have been capable of "sonic countermeasures" to avoid the hunting sonar of some other animal. And bats are the only insectivorous flying creatures we know of that are capable of hunting with sonar. Or were these perhaps pterosaurs with radar? Unfortunately, we do not have fossil evidence that can prove or disprove these hypotheses, and until the next find, we can only imagine. . . . And in imagining we turn to a completely altered planet where, paradoxically, the most successful animals—the dinosaurs—were unknowingly struggling with the future, engaged in a battle that they would soon lose. But preceisely because they lost this battle, it is still the subject of lively debates. Let us enter, then, the world of the "biology of death"—the world of extinctions.

▼ Cretoxyrhina, 23 feet long, was one of the most dangerous predators of the Cretaceous seas. Like a modern shark, it must have been equipped with senses that gave it an enormous advantage over its competitors, such as mosasaurs and marine crocodiles.

*24
page 14
panel 2

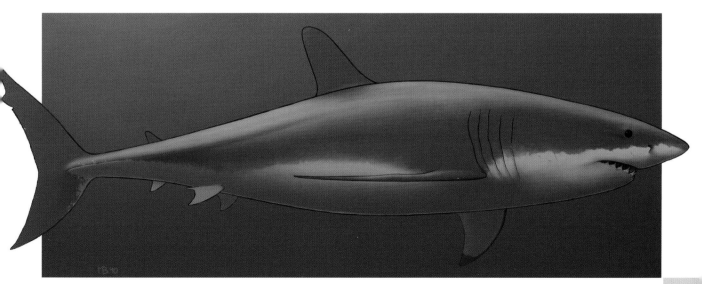

Extinction

Even with their incredible variety of forms, at a certain point in their history the dinosaurs disappeared. How was this possible? The Maastrichtian extinction, 65 million years ago (also called the K-T boundary or, more recently, the **K-Pg boundary**), has received more scientific attention than almost any other event of the past. Specialists from every discipline have felt the need to have their say about the extinction of the dinosaurs, and since many of them lack any background at all in paleontology, some of the hypotheses that have been formulated are quite far-fetched. Before looking at what we know about the events that occurred 65 million years ago and the current models that are most accepted—or rather least criticized—it is interesting to touch on some of the other theories that have been published and discussed.

First of all, most of these ideas proceed only from the fact that the non-avian dinosaurs became extinct. For the most part they ignore the extinction of many other animal groups that took place at the same time. Thus, we have seen scientists claim that skin disease might have exterminated the dinosaurs; others invoke congenital constipation instead, while their detractors "clearly demonstrate" that dinosaurs drowned in their own waste. Some have put forth the idea that the dinosaurs all committed suicide. Others have even invoked a nuclear war between the lost civilizations of Atlantis and Mu—or alien intervention! Fortunately, from the beginning there have also been more scientific, if improbable, hypotheses: for example, the idea that mammals ate all the dinosaur eggs.

Then one day an anomaly was discovered in the layers that mark the boundary between the Cretaceous (K) and the Paleogene (Pg). These layers contained a considerable quantity of iridium. Iridium is not a common element in Earth's crust, but it is common in space and in the depths of Earth's core. In the 1980s an astrophysicist—sponsored by the U.S. space missile shield program—pleaded the case for a devastating meteor impact, an asteroid of the so-called "Apollo class," at least 6 miles in diameter. This hypothesis did a good job of explaining the anomalous presence of iridium, and further research finally found "the smoking gun": a crater of vast dimensions in the Gulf of Mexico, off the coast of the Yucatán Peninsula, known as the Chicxulub Crater. The sequence of events that geologists interpreted from this crater seemed to give credence to the Alvarez hypothesis—named for the astrophysicist who proposed it. Paleontologists, however, still had doubts. Additional analyses brought to light a number of weak points in the Alvarez hypothesis, so that in the late 1990s the search for another plausible model began anew. As previously noted, iridium is not only of extra-terrestrial origin, but is also intracrustal—that is, it can be carried from inside the earth to the surface by volcanic eruptions. By the end of the twentieth century, scholars had succeeded in identifying some volcanoes of apocalyptic dimensions, for this reason known as supervolcanoes, whose enormous eruptions may have caused disasters capable of setting the K-Pg event in motion.

The K-Pg Event

What exactly took place 65 million years ago? We do not know with any certainty. What we do know is that as we approach the K-Pg boundary, fossils gradually decrease. The mass extinction affected an incredible number of life-forms, and, in fact, in terms of seriousness, this event is second only to the Permian crisis of about 250 million years ago. Non-avian dinosaurs are the most famous animal group affected by the extinction, but during the K-Pg event numerous other life-forms also died out, such as many planktonic foraminifera, ammonites, almost all marine reptiles, pterosaurs, various other invertebrates, and many plants. The catastrophe certainly must have been enormous, and it must have put a strain on vulnerable points in the ecosystem, including the food chain. In general terms, the model proposed is that some catastrophic event, practically instantaneous in effect, obscured light from the sun, a fact that in turn would have caused the loss of many **higher plants**. Based on the fossil record, the K-Pg event corresponds to a notable increase in fern spores and a collapse in the pollens of higher plants. It is possible that the damage to flora was also felt by phytoplankton, and this obviously would have set in motion a disaster in the seas. Without the mainstay of

▼ Halley's Comet (below and lower right), the most famous of the comets that are visible from Earth at predictable intervals. (Halley passes by every 76 years.) These photos were shot during its last approach, in 1986. Halley's Comet is well known, and has been considered a portent of disasters; for example, it appears in the famous Bayeux Tapestry, depicting the Norman invasion of England.

▲ A satellite photo of the Meteor Crater in Arizona. This famous impact site, approximately 4,000 feet across, was created by a meteorite only about 65 feet wide that crashed into Earth around 49,000 years ago.

The 1980 eruption of Mount St. Helens, in Washington State. Volcanic eruptions can cause miles and miles of damage, as we can see from the classical ruins at Herculaneum and Pompeii in Italy. Eruptions can bring to the surface elements not normally present in the earth's crust, such as iridium. (photo: U.S. Geological Survey)

Satellite photos of Lake Toba, in Indonesia, showing what are thought to be the remains of a super-volcano that last erupted approximately 74,000 years ago.

the marine food chains, life in the sea would have become almost unsustainable, and extinctions would have followed. Such a disaster would be magnified on land, because terrestrial life depends on the marine ecosystem and also on plants. For all practical purposes, with the extinction of flora, fauna would have gradually disappeared, and in the end a series of effects were triggered that led to the loss of nearly 50 percent of life-forms on Earth (while the Permian crisis, according to some estimates, eliminated 93 percent of life-forms). This much we know; but what we still need to find

out, to give us at least a general picture of the event, is the cause—or, more likely, the causes. If we take another look at what was happening at the end of the Cretaceous, we realize that the circumstances were favorable for extinctions to occur. The Atlantic Ocean opened up, setting in motion a radical climatic change. Seasonal variations became more pronounced: instead of alternating wet and dry seasons, there was now spring, summer, fall, and winter. Terrestrial flora changed appreciably, with the appearance and spread of not only flowering plants but also grasses *25. There were enormous volcanic eruptions—for example, in the Ring of Fire surrounding the Pacific Ocean, individual supervolcanoes, and the massive Deccan lava flows that occurred when India and Asia collided. Certain mountain chains rose up—the Alps and the Himalayas, for example. And finally, there was at least one "alien" catastrophe—that is, at least one impact with an extraterrestrial body (or two, if Chatterjee's hypothesis is correct). With all these disasters, extinctions were almost unavoidable. Thus, there wasn't a single cause, as people normally want to believe, but more likely an interaction among several causes. This is the norm in natural phenomena, and it is rare for a disaster of such proportions to have a single impetus. However, to understand why multiple interacting causes are more likely than a single one, we need to examine the debate on extinctions in greater depth.

Mass Extinctions

Thus far we have spoken of both individual extinctions and mass extinction. Now let's try to understand the difference. Generally, the term *extinction* is used when a phyletic line (a particular line of descent) terminates—that is, when a plant or animal's evolutionary line ends without leaving descendants. Imagine unwinding a long ball of string, then cutting it at a certain point. The cut represents extinction—as in the myths of the ancient Greeks and Vikings in which some sympathetic goddess had the task of cutting the thread of a human life when its time had come to an end. Extinction, as they say, is forever, meaning that once the thread is cut an extinct form never again returns. But, however terrible, the disappearance of a single phyletic line is not a crisis. Such a disappearance is known as "background extinction," and it is such a common phenomenon that it is even necessary for evolution. Yet there have been at least six catastrophic events that have resulted in much more than just some background extinctions. When an extinction is "instantaneous" in geological terms (that is, when it takes place over some thousands of years, or even a couple of million years), involves many species simultaneously, and occurs over at least half the entire globe, it is called a mass extinction, and this represents

▲ An alleged image of a "modern dinosaur" eating a hippopotamus. Such images are popular among fans of zoological science-fiction, but serious cryptozoologists normally reject the idea of dinosaurs that survived extinction. (source: L. Rossi)

*25
page 14
panel 4

a much more serious crisis. Earth has witnessed many mass extinctions, and depending on their extent, scientists divide them into major, intermediate, and lesser extinctions. We currently know of only one event classified as a major extinction, and that is the aforementioned Permian crisis. Since the Permian extinction entailed the near-total disappearance of life, it truly deserves this classification. Then there are at least five intermediate extinctions, and one of these—the largest—is the K-Pg event. There are various lesser mass extinctions; for example, the one that involved the glacial fauna of Europe at the end of the **Würm glacial stage**, approximately 10,000 years ago, was a minor event.

So how is it possible to tell from the geological record whether we are looking at a mass extinction or only some background extinctions? The answer is not very simple, because it involves a particular phenomenon that I have always found difficult to explain to students, known as the "Signor-Lipps effect."

Practically speaking, we know that there was a background extinction when we find fossil X in

▲ A rare image of a thylacine (Australian marsupial wolf), one of many animals that have become extinct due to man-made causes. The mechanisms of natural extinction have been altered and in some ways accelerated by the indiscriminate activities of man. The result is the almost daily disappearance of plant and animal species.

▶ Tigers, once widespread from Africa to China to Indonesia, are now confined to a very few habitats, having been subjected to merciless hunting. The demand for tiger amulets, furs, and trophies has brought the majestic cat to the brink of extinction.

certain layers, and then no longer find it in later layers. If, instead of fossil X, we are studying an entire fossil community—an assemblage of fossils—it becomes harder to define an extinction because some of the fossils in that community may be more fragile, or environmental conditions may have changed, causing some of them to disappear. The fossil record is an incomplete picture at best, and so it is difficult to establish such patterns. Generally, though, as we approach an extinction event, fossils tend to gradually decrease in number. The problem, however, is that as we get closer to the event, our sample size gets smaller. Think about it: say we dig down through 30 feet of earth and find a given quantity of fossils. If we dig down through only 3 feet, will we find the same number of fossils, or will we find fewer? The answer is clearly "fewer," since if the amount of sediment in which we are digging is reduced, then the likelihood of finding a fossil diminishes. This is the Signor-Lipps effect— namely, the more precisely we try to pinpoint the boundary of a mass extinction event, the more the fossil sample decreases, because the amount of sediment to be excavated decreases. This compli-

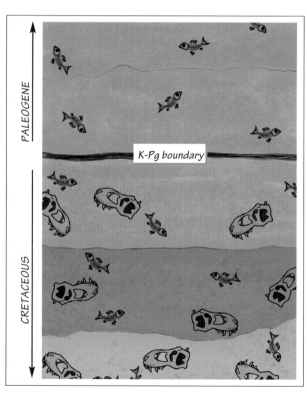

▲ The Signor-Lipps effect in action. As one approaches a boundary, the quantity of sediment available for excavation decreases, and thus so does the number of fossils. This decrease is gradual, and so any extinction event appears gradual to us. In reality, we will never know how rapid or slow mass extinctions have been.

▲ Sometimes a volcanic eruption—but also, increasingly, pollution—can cause acid rain. It has an immediate and disastrous effect on plant life and can cause local extinctions of animals as well. The K-Pg event may have involved acid rain.

cates things considerably for the paleontologists who are researching an extinction.

Nevertheless, circumstances do exist in which, despite the Signor-Lipps effect, it becomes truly difficult to confuse a lack of data with a catastrophic event. For example, as we approach the K-Pg event there is a gradual disappearance of not only dinosaurs—all dinosaurs—but also pterosaurs, plesiosaurs, mosasaurs, ammonites, globotruncana, and globorotalia (the latter two are groups of foraminifera). So something is clearly not right. If we then discover that all these disappearances occurred simultaneously over nearly the entire planet, then it is clear that we are faced with a mass extinction, and one of significant proportions.

Things do not end here, however, and in fact the fun has only just begun. Now we can see what happens in a "generalized" mass extinction. The first thing that occurs is the collapse of the food chain, as we have noted. This happens because certain fundamental taxa that support other taxa die out. For example, imagine a mass death of present-day phytoplankton. All the zooplankton that use phytoplankton as food die immediately, simply because they no longer have

anything to eat. As a result, two things happen. On the one hand, what is called recruitment—that is, generational replacement—ceases, because a great many fish at the larval stage live in the zooplankton. When these die, they obviously never become the next generation of adults, and thus will never produce new larvae. On the other hand, all the large animals that live on zooplankton—for example, filter-feeding whales or sharks—are unable to find food and starve. With only three changes, unimaginable damage has been done to the marine food chains. And this is just the beginning. Many, many species of fish also live on zooplankton, and they in turn are food for other fish species. The sea begins to empty out. Then all the coastal birds that feed on fish no longer find food, and they begin to die out. All the terrestrial predators that feed on the coastal birds are forced into extinction. And as if this were not enough, the disappearance of phytoplankton causes a serious decrease in the oxygen levels in the air, and thus many terrestrial plants suffer. Their disappearance leads to the disappearance of herbivores, which in turn does irreparable damage to carnivores. By now you get the picture.

This is an extremely brief summary of what normally happens during a biological crisis of planetary significance, and it all leads to a mass extinction. Things are even more complex when we focus on the details. Let's say two species struggle for a depleted resource. One species wins, and the other is thus destroyed. But then a third species unexpectedly shows up, and it in turn destroys the previously victorious species, while the resources further diminish and also damage this newcomer. These cycles are well-known mechanisms, not only in nature, but also in human economics, and they are usually self-regulating because the damage caused keeps the cycle in motion, as it were, always leading to new configurations of competition.

Beyond these basic principles, no one is really sure how and why extinctions function. There are various models that try to explain the generalized methods and causality of an extinction. Charles Darwin, for example, maintained that direct competition is the primary cause of extinction. According to the scholar Leigh Van Valen, however, the possibility of extinction in a given group remains constant over time—that is, all living groups always have the same potential to die out. Van Valen suggests, moreover, that balance in nature keeps things functioning, but that balance requires constant development; if the balance is changed—in the course of the constant development—the natural system can go to pieces and an extinction occurs. Thus he proposes the model of the Red Queen's race (as in *Alice in Wonderland*), in which you have to run (develop) as fast as you can to stay in the same place (maintain balance). Other authors are convinced that extinctions have exclusively **abiotic causes**. Finally, some think that there is a competition mechanism among organisms, so that the appearance of new forms provokes the extinction of old ones, and an ecological niche can be reoccupied only if the species that fills it is swept away by external factors. In short, we know that catastrophes occur, but we still are not clear about how they function to balance or renew the ecosystem.

From the standpoint of paleontology, the situation is further complicated by the incompleteness of our data. We have seen in the previous volumes that what the paleontologist sees in the fossil record is only a fraction of the prehistoric ecosys-

tem, because most of the plants and animals—those that were not fossilized—are missing. So it is by no means easy to fully understand the dynamics of extinction. For example, one of the biggest questions surrounding the crisis of the Late Cretaceous is why the mosasaurs, the gigantic marine lizards, went extinct. Some forms ate ammonites, and so died out when the latter did. But what happened to the mosasaurs that ate fish, since fish did not all die out? Things become complicated when we see that not only sharks, but also other fish-eating marine reptiles, such as Dyrosauridae (marine crocodiles) easily survived the crisis. Why did these animals escape extinction while the mosasaurs did not? We are continually reconsidering problems of this kind as our knowledge gradually increases. As one question is answered, three more appear. As a paleontologist once said, the problem with mass extinctions is not figuring out which species became extinct, but rather why others did not.

In conclusion, we may never know what happened at the end of the Cretaceous, but we do know that there was no single cause for one of the greatest mass extinctions in the planet's history. And thanks to studies on extinction, we also know that the scenarios presented by nature are never simple or linear. On the contrary, they are the result of complex interactions of structures that are themselves complex, including living creatures, environments, and ecosystems.

In any case, like it or not, in the end the lords of evolution, the non-avian dinosaurs, did die out. They disappeared, clearly not without a trace, but nonetheless leaving behind a great void. Time went on, the world changed, and new creatures appeared to fill this void. The first to do so were the avian dinosaurs themselves, some of which abandoned the sky and adapted to living on land, like their glorious ancestors. These swift-footed predators, like *Phorusrachus* or *Dinornis*, evolved into gigantic forms, capable of unleashing terror among packs of early mammals. But they too would have to yield to the ultimate power of evolution, to creatures that, a few million years earlier, had existed only in the shadow of the dinosaurs: mammals. And this, as they say, is truly another story. And who knows, in the very near future, we may meet again, around a virtual fire, to tell that story. After all, the longest journey is the one taken with the mind.

GLOSSARY

abiotic causes: sources of change that do not depend on living creatures, but that rely exclusively on physical, chemical, or geological phenomena.

higher plants: angiosperms (flowering plants) and gymnosperms (conifers and others). Higher plants have a vascular structure capable of transporting water, minerals, and products of photosynthesis to various parts of the plant.

K-Pg boundary: the line between the Cretaceous period (K) and the Paleogene period (Pg), marking the point at which a mass extinction occurred.

ratites: family of running, flightless birds to which the ostrich and the cassowary belong.

trabeculated: having internal supporting rods. Hollow bones may be trabeculated.

Würm glacial stage: the last Ice Age event, approximately 10,000 years ago, in Europe. The name is derived from a tributary of the Danube River.

DINOSAURS

1 THE JOURNEY: *Plateosaurus*

We follow the path of a great herd of *Plateosaurus* from the sea—populated by ichthyosaurs—through the desert and mountains, to their nesting places. Their trek takes place beneath skies plied by the pterosaur *Eudimorphodon*, and under the watchful eye of the predator *Liliensternus*.

We discover what life was like on our planet during the Triassic period, and how the dinosaurs evolved.

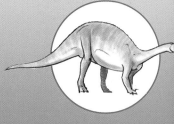

2 A JURASSIC MYSTERY: *Archaeopteryx*

What killed the colorfully plumed *Archaeopteryx*? Against the backdrop of a great tropical storm, we search for the perpetrator among the animals that populate a Jurassic lagoon, such as the small carnivore *Juravenator*, the pterosaur *Pterodactylus*, crocodiles, and prehistoric fish.

We discover how dinosaurs spread throughout the world in the Jurassic period and learned to fly, and how a paleontologist interprets fossils.

3 THE HUNTING PACK: *Allosaurus*

We see how life unfolds in a herd of *Allosaurus* led by an enormous and ancient male, as they hunt *Camarasaurus* and the armored *Stegosaurus* in groups, look after their young, and struggle amongst themselves. A young and powerful *Allosaurus* forces its way into the old leader's harem. How will the confrontation end?

We discover one of the most spectacular ecosystems in the history of the Earth: the Morrison Formation in North America.